THE LONGEST CHRISTMAS LIST EVER

by Gregg & Evan Spiridellis

with John Nugent, Brandon Scott, and Ian Worrel

Hyperion Books for Children

New York

For our beautiful, perfect, wonderful children

First Edition
This book is set in St. Nicholas.
1 3 5 7 9 10 8 6 4 2
ISBN-13: 978-1-4231-0193-2
ISBN-10: 1-4231-0193-6

Printed in Hong Kong
Reinforced binding

Library of Congress Cataloging-in-Publication Data on file.

Visit www.hyperionbooksforchildren.com

On Christmas morning, not so long ago,
In a house on a hill, all covered in snow,
Asleep in his bed was a little boy, Trevor,
Who dreamed it would be the best Christmas ever. . . .

His parents were snoring at 5:45,
When Trevor *crashed* into their bed with a dive.
"WAKE UP! WAKE UP! Ya gotta come see!
All of the presents stacked under the tree!"

He ran out of the bedroom and bounced down the stairs.
There wasn't a doubt that St. Nick had been there.

"A scooter!
A gamebox!
Two trucks that collide!"

He tore open gifts . . . and tossed them aside.

Then it suddenly hit him,
The one thing he'd missed . . .
"A fluffy brown puppy was not on my list!"

Trevor knew what to do
And he didn't postpone it.
"I'll start next year's Christmas list
This very moment!"

He snatched up a notepad,
A pen, and a seat,
And started his list
At the top of the sheet.

At first he thought small, like lizards and trolls.
But quickly his list spiraled out of control . . .

A remote-controlled plane with a camera inside!

An invisible robot that's easy to hide!

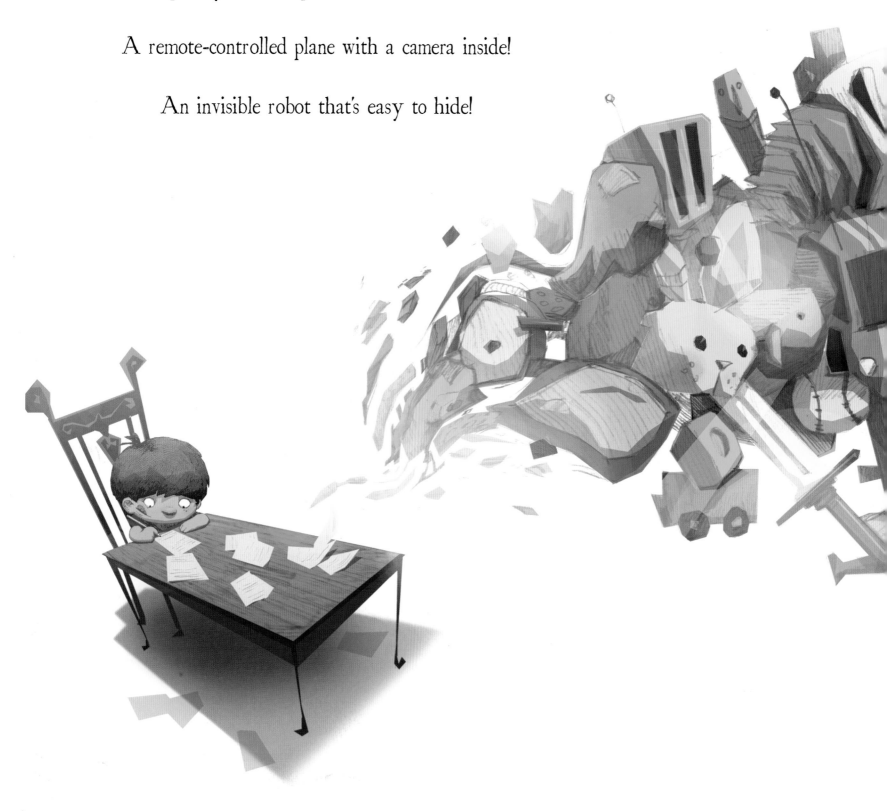

Binocular glasses with night-vision mode!

A rip-roaring go-kart to tear down the road!

Suction-cup shoes to walk on the ceiling!

A nuclear jet pack, now that sounds appealing!

Trevor kept writing, day in and day out.
His pads filled up boxes, now scattered about!

They spilled out of his room and into the hall,
Then snaked down the stairway and climbed up the wall!

By spring Trevor's list stretched 500 feet

By summer it made its way onto Main Street.

By fall it was two blocks beyond the bookstore . . .

By winter it reached the post-office door!

Trevor stepped up to the counter inside.
"I must mail my list," he said with great pride.
But the mailman let out a hoot and a holler,
"To send this whole list would cost SIX TRILLION DOLLARS!"

Trevor then emptied his little coin box:

A nickel,
Two dimes,
And three dirty rocks.

"One bit of advice, if you've got just a quarter.
Go back to your list, and make it much shorter!"

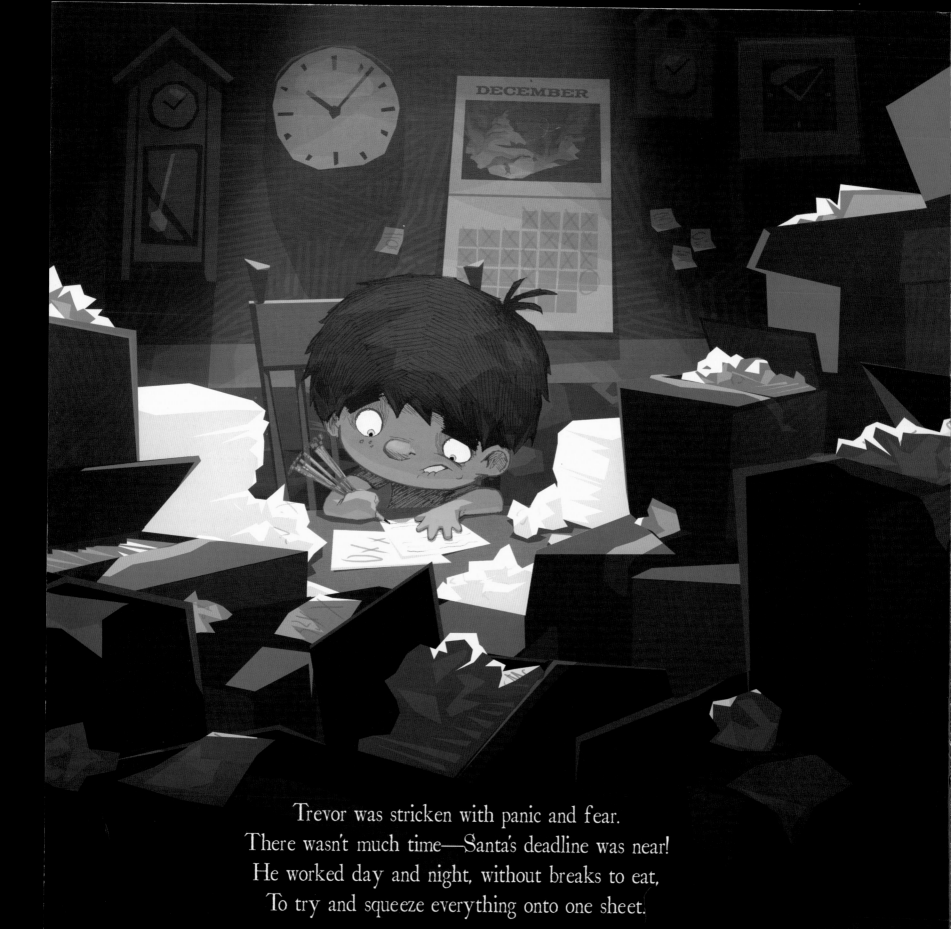

Trevor was stricken with panic and fear.
There wasn't much time—Santa's deadline was near!
He worked day and night, without breaks to eat,
To try and squeeze everything onto one sheet.

But time, it was short, and his letter tremendous.
He missed Santa's deadline, and felt plain horrendous.

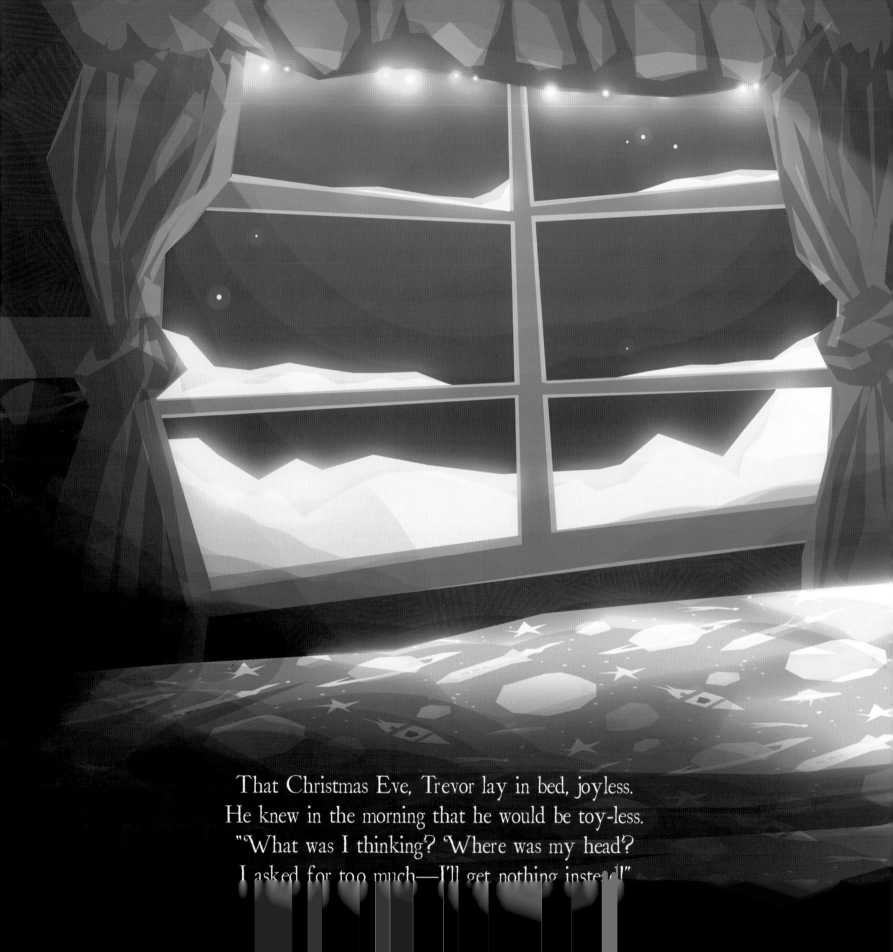

That Christmas Eve, Trevor lay in bed, joyless.
He knew in the morning that he would be toy-less.
"What was I thinking? Where was my head?
I asked for too much—I'll get nothing instead."

In the morning he trudged down the stairs without glee,
Certain there'd be nothing under the tree.
But Mom and Dad must have sent Santa a letter . . .
'Cuz a puppy appeared and POUNCED little Trevor!

They rolled on the floor, took turns giving chase.
Trevor squealed in delight at the licks on his face!
His prior mistake was now perfectly clear:
It takes love—not toys—to bring Christmas cheer.